# HORRiD HENRY
## and the
## Mega-Mean
## Time Machine

# HORRID HENRY

## and the
## Mega-Mean
## Time Machine

Francesca Simon
*Illustrated by* Tony Ross

Orion
Children's Books

*Horrid Henry and the Mega-Mean Time Machine* first appeared in the
storybook of the same name first published in Great Britain in 2005
by Orion Children's Books
This edition first published in Great Britain in 2016
by Hodder and Stoughton

5 7 9 10 8 6 4

Text copyright Francesca Simon, 2005
Illustrations copyright Tony Ross, 2016

A CIP catalogue record for this book
is available from the British Library.

ISBN 978 1 4440 1602 4

Printed and bound in China

The paper and board used in this book are from well-managed forests
and other responsible sources.

Orion Children's Books
An imprint of
Hachette Children's Group
Part of Hodder & Stoughton
Carmelite House
50 Victoria Embankment
London EC4Y 0DZ

An Hachette UK Company
www.hachette.co.uk

www.hachettechildrens.co.uk

*For Louis*

There are many more
**Horrid Henry** Early Reader books available.

For a complete list visit:
www.orionchildrensbooks.com
or
www.horridhenry.co.uk

# Contents

# Chapter 1

Horrid Henry flicked the switch.
The time machine whirred.

Dials spun.

Buttons pulsed.

Latches locked.

# Horrid Henry Time Traveller
was ready for blast off!

Now, where to go, where to go?
Dinosaurs, thought Henry. Yes!
Henry loved dinosaurs. He would
love to stalk a few Tyrannosaurus
Rexes as they rampaged through
the primordial jungle.

But what about King Arthur and the Knights of the Round Table? "Arise, Sir Henry," King Arthur would say, booting Lancelot out of his chair.

"Sure thing, King," Sir Henry would reply, twirling his sword. "Out of my way, worms!"

Or what about the siege of Troy?
Heroic Henry, that's who he'd be,
the fearless fighter dashing about
doing daring deeds.

Tempting,
thought Henry.
Very tempting.

Wait a sec, what about visiting
the future, where school was banned
and parents had to do whatever
their children told them?
Where everyone had their own
spaceship and ate sweets for dinner.

And where King Henry the Horrible
ruled supreme, chopping off the head
of anyone who dared to say no
to him.

To the future,
thought Henry, setting the dial.

# Chapter 2

Bang!

Pow!

Henry braced himself for the jolt
into hyperspace –

10

9

8

7

6…

"Henry, it's my turn."
Horrid Henry ignored the
alien's whine.

**5**

**4**

**3**

"Henry! If you don't share
I'm going to tell Mum."

# Aaaarrrrggghhhhhh.

The Time Machine juddered to a halt.
Henry climbed out.

"Go away, Peter," said Henry. "You're spoiling everything."

"But it's my turn."

# "Go away!"

"Mum said we could both play with the box," said Peter. "We could cut out windows, make a little house, paint flowers…"

"NO!" screeched Henry.

"But…" said Peter.
He stood in the sitting room,
holding his scissors and crayons.

"Don't you touch my box!"
hissed Henry.

"I will if I want to," said Peter.
"And it's not yours."

Henry had no right to boss him
around, thought Peter. He'd been
waiting such a long time for his
turn. Well, he wasn't waiting any
longer. He'd start cutting out
a window this minute.
Peter got out his scissors.

# "Stop!

It's a time machine, you toad!"
shrieked Henry.

# Chapter 3

Peter paused.
Peter gasped.
Peter stared at the huge
cardboard box.

A time machine?
# A time machine?
How could it be a time machine?

"It is not," said Peter.

"Is too," said Henry.

"But it's made of cardboard,"
said Peter. "And the
washing machine came in it."

Henry sighed.
"Don't you know anything?
If it looked like a time machine
everyone would try to steal it.
It's a time machine in disguise."

Peter looked at the time machine.
On the one hand he didn't believe
Henry for one minute. This was just
one of Henry's tricks. Peter was a

# hundred
# million
# billion

percent certain Henry was lying.

On the other hand, what if Henry
was telling the truth for once
and there was a real time machine
in his sitting room?

"If it is a time machine I want
to have a go," said Peter.

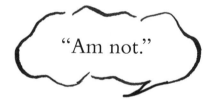
"You can't.
You're too young,"
said Henry.

"Am not."

"Are too."

Perfect Peter stuck out his bottom lip.
"I don't believe you anyway."

Horrid Henry was outraged.
"Okay, I'll prove it. I'll go to
the future right now.
Stand back. Don't move."
Horrid Henry leapt into the box
and closed the lid.

The Time Machine began to
shudder and shake.

Then everything was still for
a very long time.

Perfect Peter didn't know what to do.
What if Henry was gone – forever?
What if he were stuck in the future?

I could have his room, thought Peter.

I could watch whatever
I wanted on telly.

I could...

Suddenly the box tipped over and
Horrid Henry staggered out.
"Wh-wh-where am I?"
he stuttered.

Then he collapsed on the floor.

# Chapter 4

Peter stared at Henry.
Henry stared wildly at Peter.

"I've been to the future!"
gasped Henry, panting. "It was
amazing. Wow. I met my great-great-
great-grandson. He still lives in this
house. And he looks just like me."

"So he's ugly," muttered Peter.

"What – did – you – say?"
hissed Henry.

"Nothing," said Peter quickly.
He didn't know what to think.
"Is this a trick, Henry?"

"Course it isn't," said Henry.
"And just for that I won't let you
have a go."

"I can if I want to," said Peter.

"You keep away from my time
machine," said Henry.
"One wrong move and you'll get
blasted into the future."

Perfect Peter walked a few steps
towards the time machine.

Then he paused.
"What's it like in the future?"

"Boys wear dresses," said Horrid Henry. "And lipstick. People talk Ugg language. You'd probably like it. Everyone just eats vegetables."

"Really?"

"And kids have loads of homework."

Perfect Peter loved homework.

## "Ooohh."

This Peter had to see. Just in case
Henry was telling the truth.
"I'm going to the future and you
can't stop me," said Peter.

"Go ahead," said Henry.
Then he snorted. "You can't go
looking like that!"

"Why not?" said Peter.

"'Cause everyone will laugh at you."

Perfect Peter hated people
laughing at him.

"Why?"

"Because to them you'll look weird."

Are you sure you really want
to go to the future?"

"Yes," said Peter.

"Are you sure you're sure?"

"YES," said Peter.

"Then I'll get you ready,"
said Henry solemnly.

"Thank you, Henry," said Peter.
Maybe he'd been wrong about Henry.
Maybe going to the future had turned
him into a nice brother.
Horrid Henry dashed out of the
sitting room.

Perfect Peter felt a quiver
of excitement. The future.
What if Henry really was telling
the truth?

# Chapter 5

Horrid Henry returned carrying a large wicker basket. He pulled out an old red dress of Mum's, some lipstick, and a black frothy drink.

"Here, put this on," said Henry.
Perfect Peter put on the dress.
It dragged onto the floor.
"Now, with a bit of lipstick,"
said Horrid Henry, applying big blobs
of red lipstick all over Peter's face,
"you'll fit right in."

"Perfect," he said, standing back to admire his handiwork. "You look just like a boy from the future."

"Okay," said Perfect Peter.

"Now listen carefully," said Henry.
"When you arrive, you won't be
able to speak the language unless you
drink this bibble babble drink.

Take this with you and drink it
when you get there."
Henry held out the frothy black drink
from his Dungeon Drink Kit.
Peter took it.

"You can now enter the
time machine."

Peter obeyed.
His heart was pounding.

"Don't get out until the time machine has stopped moving completely. Then count to twenty-five, and open the hatch very, very slowly. You don't want a bit of you in the twenty-third century, and the rest here in the twenty-first. Good luck."

Henry swirled the box round
and round and round.
The drink sloshed on the floor.

Then everything was still.

# Chapter 6

Peter's head was spinning.
He counted to twenty-five,
then crept out.

He was in the sitting room of
a house that looked just like his.
A boy wearing a bathrobe and silver
waggly antennae with his face painted
in blue stripes stood in front of him.

"Ugg?" said the strange boy.

"Henry?" said Peter.

"Uggg uggg bleuch ble bloop,"
said the boy.

"Uggg uggg," said Peter uncertainly.

"Uggh uggh drink ugggh,"
said the boy, pointing to
Peter's bibble babble drink.
Peter drank the few drops
which were left.

"I'm Zog," said Zog. "Who are you?"

"I'm Peter," said Peter.

"Ahhhhh! Welcome! You must be my great-great-great-uncle Peter. Your very nice brother Henry told me all about you when he visited me from the past."

"Oh, what did he say?" said Peter.

"That you were an ugly toad."

"I am not," said Peter.
"Wait a minute," he added
suspiciously. "Henry said that boys
wore dresses in the future."

"They do," said Zog quickly.
"I'm a girl."

"Oh," said Peter. He gasped.
Henry would never in a million years
say he was a girl. Not even if he were
being poked with red hot pokers.

Could it be…

Peter looked around.
"This looks just like my sitting room."

Zog snorted.
"Of course it does, Uncle Pete.
This is now the Peter Museum.
You're famous in the future.
Everything has been kept exactly
as it was."

Peter beamed.
He was famous in the future.
He always knew he'd be famous.
A Peter Museum! He couldn't wait to
tell Spotless Sam and Tidy Ted.

There was just one more thing…

"What about Henry?" he asked.
"Is he famous too?"

"Nah," said Zog smoothly.
"He's known as What's-His-Name,
Peter's older brother."

Ahh.
Peter swelled with pride.
Henry was in his lowly place,
at last.

That proved it.
He'd really travelled to the future!

# Chapter 7

Peter looked out of the window. Strange how the future didn't look so different from his own time.

Zog pointed.
"Our spaceships," he announced.
Peter stared.
Spaceships looked just like cars.

"Why aren't they flying?" said Peter.

"Only at night time," said Zog.
"You can either drive 'em or fly 'em."

"Wow," said Peter.

"Don't you have spaceships?"
said Zog.

"No," said Peter. "Cars."

"I didn't know they had cars in
olden days," said Zog. "Do you have

blitzkatrons

and

zappersnappers?"

"No," said Peter. "What…"

The front door slammed.

Mum walked in.
She stared at Peter.
"What on earth…"

"Don't be scared," said Peter.
"I'm Peter. I come from the past.
I'm your great great great
grandfather."

Mum looked at Peter.
Peter looked at Mum.
"Why are you wearing my dress?"
said Mum.

"It's not one of yours, silly," said Peter.
"It belonged to my mum."

"I see," said Mum.

"Come on, Uncle Pete," said Zog quickly, taking Peter firmly by the arm. "I'll show you our supersonic hammock in the garden."

"Okay, Zog," said Peter happily.

Mum beamed.

"It's so lovely to see you playing
nicely with your brother, Henry."
Perfect Peter stood still.

"What did you call him?"

"Henry," said Mum.

Peter felt a chill.
"So his name's not Zog?
And he's not a girl?"

"Not the last time I looked,"
said Mum.

"And this house isn't . . .
the Peter Museum?"

Mum glared at Henry.
"Henry! Have you been teasing
Peter again?"

"Ha ha tricked you!" shrieked Henry. "Na Na Ne Nah Nah, wait till I tell everybody!"

"NO!" squealed Peter. "Nooooooo!" How could he have believed his horrible brother?

"Henry! You horrid boy!
Go to your room!
No TV for the rest of the day,"
said Mum.

But Horrid Henry didn't care.
The Mega–Mean Time Machine
would go down in history as his
greatest trick ever.